While his mother worked, Aladdin roamed the city streets,
lost in daydreams of untold riches. Until, one day...

"Aladdin!" cried a strange man. "At last, I have found you.
I am your long-lost uncle, Abanazar."

"From now on, I will take care of you!" declared Abanazar. "I'll dress you in silk robes and fill your pockets with gold...

...but in return, I need you to do a little something for ME."

Intrigued, Aladdin agreed.

Retold by Susanna Davidson

Illustrated by Lorena Alvarez

Long, long ago, when flying carpets still whizzed over desert cities and dragons roared in mountain caves, there lived a young, lazy good-for-nothing boy, named

Aladdin.

Abanazar led Aladdin deep into the
mountains, and then deeper still.
He conjured a fire and muttered
strange spells. There was a sudden
CRASH of thunder
and a trapdoor appeared.

"Don't run away!" said Abanazar, grabbing Aladdin. "Treasure lies beneath this door, along with a lamp. Fetch them for me!"

Trembling with fear, Aladdin crept down, down, down into the darkness.

At the end of the tunnel lay a garden, shining with jewels.
At first, Aladdin gazed in astonishment. Then he picked up
the lamp and stuffed his pockets with gems and gold.

But when he tried to climb back, the jewels weighed
him down. He called out to Abanazar.

I cannot go any further!
Please! Help me up!

"First give me the lamp!" cried Abanazar.
"And the jewels." But Aladdin was no longer sure
he trusted this man with greedy, gleaming eyes.

He shook his head and, in a rage,
Abanazar slammed the door shut.

Alone in the cold dark, Aladdin wrung his
hands and wept. One of the rings began
to crackle and sparkle until...

Whoosh!

...there, in a puff of
smoke, was a genie,
glowing green.

I am the genie of the ring.
What is your command?

"Take me home," pleaded Aladdin.
In an instant, he was back with his mother.

"Aladdin!" she cried. "Where have you been?"
So Aladdin told his tale.

"But I don't understand why Abanazar wanted this lamp," he said. As he spoke, his mother rubbed it clean and...

Whoosh!

Floating above them was a blue genie, even bigger than the first.

I am the genie of the lamp! What is your command?

"Delicious dishes on golden plates!" laughed Aladdin.
"Silk dresses and flowing scarves," added his mother.

From that day on, Aladdin and his mother
wanted for nothing. They lived like royalty.

They dressed in the finest silks and even
had tea with the Emperor. And there, in the
palace gardens, Aladdin saw Princess Moon
Flower, the Emperor's beautiful daughter.

Aladdin fell instantly in love. He went to the Emperor with bowls piled high with gold and jewels. "May I marry your daughter?" he asked.

"You have my blessing," said the Emperor. "But first, you must ask the princess."
"I do wish to marry Aladdin," said Princess Moon Flower, smiling.

"Then we'll need a new home!" Aladdin declared.
And the genie whisked up a palace with
a thousand windows, its walls a dazzling blue.

On their wedding day, Aladdin and the princess
rode through the streets on prancing white horses,
as the crowds clapped and cheered.

But watching from the shadows was the wicked Abanazar.
"Aladdin has stolen my treasure! And now he's married
the princess! I'll have my revenge..."

He waited until Aladdin went out,
then he crept into the palace and
rubbed the magic lamp.

I am the genie of the lamp!
What is your command?

"Take us to Africa!" snarled Abanazar.
"Bring the palace too!"

Aladdin returned to find his wife and home had vanished.
He despaired... until he remembered the genie of the ring.

"Please!" he begged.
"Bring back the princess."

I am not as powerful as the genie of the lamp,

but I can take you to her.

In a lush garden in Africa, Aladdin was reunited with his wife.
"It was Abanazar who brought me here," she said.

Then Princess Moon Flower smiled a secret smile and, from
the folds of her dress, she brought out the magic lamp.

On Aladdin's command, the genie cast Abanazar onto
a far-flung island, so he would never trouble them again.

Then, in the palm of his hand, the genie brought Aladdin,
the princess and their palace back home again at last.

From that day on, Aladdin and Princess
Moon Flower lived happily in the palace of
a thousand windows. As for the lamp and
the ring... who knows? Perhaps they are still
there today, with the genies waiting inside.

'Aladdin' is a folk tale from the Middle East. It comes from a famous collection of Middle Eastern tales called 'A Thousand and One Nights'.

Edited by Lesley Sims
Designed by Laura Nelson Norris

First published in 2018 by Usborne Publishing Ltd., Usborne House, 83-85 Saffron Hill, London EC1N 8RT, England. www.usborne.com Copyright © 2018, 2017 Usborne Publishing Ltd.